I0788530

My Love Story

How Latin Dancing Changed My Life

Jaime Jesus

Dedication

To my beloved twin brother, Nestor Manuelian.

You were a force of rhythm and light,

guiding countless souls into the embrace of Latin dance.

I will forever treasure the gift of witnessing your magic, the way you changed lives, simply by being you.

Though you've gone beyond the music,

Your spirit moves our community and will change lives forever

Acknowledgment

To all those past and present who helped shape the person I am today in the Latin Dance industry. Thank you for opening doors when I was just beginning, for believing in me, and for changing my life through the power of Latin dance. A special thanks to Marcia Percival, my mentor, and the one who set me on this incredible journey. Your guidance lit the path that led me here.

Contents

Hi, I'm Nathan

When I first decided to get into Latin dancing, I thought choosing a dance school would be the easiest part. Spoiler alert, it wasn't.

My name's Nathan, and like a lot of people, I started dancing because I wanted to feel more confident, meet new people, and have fun. But when I began searching for schools, I quickly got overwhelmed. There were so many options: Salsa, Bachata, Cuban, Mambo, LA style, Dominican style… it was a whole world I didn't even know existed.

At first, I just picked the one closest to home. It was fine, but something didn't click. So I tried another. And another. Along the way, I learned what really mattered, things like the vibe of the community, how the teachers made you feel, whether the classes were welcoming for beginners, and how often they offered socials to actually practice.

It took me a while, but eventually I found my people. The school I chose felt like home. The instructors were passionate, the dancers were friendly, and I left every class buzzing with energy. Looking back, I wish someone had helped me figure it out sooner.

So now, I'm putting together a little guide to help other newbies find the right dance school, without all the guesswork I went through.

Follow me through my journey, and discover the best quick tips no one gives you, and that are usually hard to find.

Get ready for a whole new world and community, you are in for something life-changing.

DANCE SCHOOL

NEWBIE'S GUIDE TO CHOOSING A GREAT DANCE SCHOOL

1. Define Your Dance Goals

Do you want to dance socially, professionally, or for fitness?

Are you interested in a specific style like Salsa, Bachata, Ballroom, or Hip-Hop?

2. Research Dance Styles Offered

Make sure the school teaches the style(s) you're passionate about.

Some schools specialize in Latin dances, others in classical or urban styles.

3. Check Instructor Qualifications

Look into the background and experience of the instructors.

Are they active performers, competitors, or certified teachers?

4. Attend a Trial Class or Open House

Most reputable schools offer a free or low-cost trial.

Get a feel for the teaching style, class structure, and energy of the space

5. Evaluate Class Structure

Are classes grouped by skill level?

Is there a clear progression path (Beginner > Intermediate > Advanced)?

6. Consider Class Size and Student Attention

Smaller class sizes often mean more personalized feedback.

Watch how instructors interact with students

7. Ask About Partner Rotation (for Partner Dances)

Will you need to bring a partner?

Do they rotate partners in class to improve social dancing skills?

8. Look for a Welcoming Vibe

Are the staff and students friendly and inclusive?

A positive environment helps you stay motivated and engaged.

9. Compare Prices and Packages

Are there flexible payment options (drop-ins, monthly, class packs)?

Are there any hidden fees (registration, costumes, exams)?

10. Check Reviews and Word-of-Mouth

Read Google reviews or ask local dancers about their experiences.

Personal recommendations often reveal what marketing doesn't.

My First Love

When I first stepped into the Latin dance world, I thought "Salsa is Salsa," right? Simple enough. Or so I thought.

Salsa was my first love. The music, the energy, the way it made people light up on the dance floor, it pulled me in from the very start. I signed up for my first class, and that was it. I was hooked.

But then I found out… Salsa isn't just Salsa. There's LA style (On1), New York style (On2), Cuban, Colombian, and even something called Mambo that had a whole different flavor. And that's not even touching Bachata, Kizomba, or other Latin styles floating around in the same social scene.

At first, I tried to do it all, jumping between styles, trying to keep up, feeling lost half the time. Some styles just didn't hit the same way. Others were fun, but Salsa? Salsa was home. The rhythms made sense in my body. The turn patterns excited me. The music made me feel something.

I eventually found clarity, but it took trial, error and a lot of sweaty nights. Here are some important tips for new dancers trying to figure out what style fits them.

DANCE STYLE

NEWBIE'S GUIDE TO CHOOSING A LATIN DANCE STYLE

7. Social Scene Matters

Check which styles are most popular in your area. You'll progress faster and enjoy it more if there's a strong local scene with socials, classes, and events.

8. Look at the Learning Curve

Salsa/Mambo and Samba tend to have more complex footwork and timing, while Bachata and Reggaeton can feel more accessible for beginners.

9. Match Your Personality

Love high energy and challenge? Try Salsa/Mambo or Samba.

Into feeling and flow? Go for Bachata or Kizomba.

Like power and swag? Reggaeton might be your style.

Love control and rhythm? Explore Cha Cha or Zouk.

10. Don't Stress – Start Somewhere

You don't have to commit forever. Start with what excites you most. The Latin dance world is big; you'll likely fall in love with more than one style along the way.

You Always Remember Your First

I'll never forget my first social dance.

I'd been taking Salsa classes for a few weeks and figured, Hey, I know the basic step, I've got this! So I Googled "Latin social dance near me" and picked the first one that popped up. It had a flyer with palm trees, mojitos, and people in white linen outfits. Sounded fun. Spoiler: it was not the right fit.

I walked in wearing my fresh button-up and the jeans that would later betray me (a story for another day). The room was packed with couples doing some kind of fast, circular Cuban-style Salsa I'd never seen before. The music was loud, the vibe was intense, and I had no idea where the "LA Style On1" dancing I had learned even fit into this scene.

I asked someone to dance, and she smiled politely, but after a few bars, she gently said, "Oh, you dance linear? I don't really dance LA style. I dance mostly Cuban". She was kind, but I could feel the awkward. I danced two more songs, mostly stepping on myself, and left early, trying to act like I just had "somewhere to be." I almost gave up on socials altogether.

But a week later, my instructor mentioned a local Mambo and

Salsa On1/On2 social at a different studio. Smaller crowd, friendlier vibe, and mostly dancers from my classes. I decided to give it one more shot. That night changed everything.

I knew the music. I recognized people. The dancers welcomed me in, gave me tips, smiled when I messed up, and actually enjoyed dancing with beginners. I stayed until the last song, soaked in sweat but grinning like a maniac. It was the first time I felt like I belonged in this world.

But here's the twist: I never forgot that first Cuban-style social. And instead of avoiding it forever, I decided to learn Cuban Salsa too.

I figured, Why not open more doors? Now, I can enjoy both worlds: the linear smoothness of what I'd learned, and the playful, rhythmic energy of Cuban Salsa. It's doubled the fun and doubled my dance family.

So find the right social first, and maybe even a little nudge to try styles outside your comfort zone.

LATIN DANCE SOCIAL

NEWBIE'S GUIDE TO CHOOSING A GREAT LATIN SOCIAL

1. Music is King

Check if the DJ plays a good mix of Salsa, Bachata, and maybe some Kizomba or Zouk, depending on your taste. A great playlist keeps the energy flowing all night.

2. Floor Quality Matters

A smooth, clean dance floor (preferably wooden or sprung) makes a world of difference. Avoid sticky, slippery, or uneven surfaces.

3. Friendly & Welcoming Crowd

A social where people are approachable and open to dancing with everyone (not just their group) is a winner.

4. Skill Level Balance

It's nice to have a mix of beginner to advanced dancers. That way, you get to challenge yourself and still have fun.

5. Location & Parking

Is it easy to get to? Is there safe and accessible parking or public transport nearby? Convenience helps keep you coming back.

6. Good Vibes & Ambience

Lighting, venue layout, décor, and general atmosphere should invite you to relax and enjoy. Some venues feel like a party, others like a practice—choose your vibe

7. Hosts & Organisers Matter

Are the organisers warm, experienced, and involved in the scene? Great hosts set the tone and make sure everyone feels included.

8. Safety First Especially for late-night socials, check if the venue feels safe, is in a good area, and takes care of its patrons.

9. Consistency & Reputation

Socials that run regularly and have a good rep often provide a more reliable experience. Ask around or check reviews.

10. Extras & Surprises

Do they offer shows, animations, mini-workshops, or themes? These can spice up your night and offer more than just social dancing. Want me to turn this into a graphic or promo post for LDA or a specific event?

Hole in One

Oh yeah, the night I learned exactly why what you wear and how you smell matters when you dance.

I had no clue there was such a thing as "dance clothes." I'd show up in jeans, sneakers, maybe a button-up if I was feeling extra. I figured, "If I can move in it, I'm good." Spoiler: I was very wrong.

One Friday night, I hit up this big social. The room was packed, the music was fire, the energy was wild, and I was feeling myself. I asked this stunning dancer to join me; she looked like she'd been dancing forever, but I was riding that newbie high, so I went for it.

We were mid-song, spinning, turning, connecting, everything was flowing. I was sweating like crazy, but pushing through it to look cool. I noticed a moment where she gently pulled back a little during a close move. I thought maybe I misstepped. Nope. It hit me a second later: Oh God… was that me? Yeah. Turns out, dancing hard in heavy denim and a cotton shirt with no ventilation is a one-way ticket to Funk Town.

To make matters worse, my breath? Not helping. Note to self:

water and mints are friends. Determined to recover, I went big. Cross-body lead, double spin, snappy stop, and RRRIIIPPPP.

Yup. My jeans split. Loud, unmistakable, and perfectly timed with the beat. We froze, then we laughed. I laughed too, but half mortified, half relieved that at least we were both cool about it. I wrapped my jacket around my waist like I was covering a crime scene and finished the song, barely. I nodded, bowed, and got out of there fast.

That night was a turning point.

After that, I dove deep into the world of dancewear: stretchy pants that looked normal, breathable shirts that let me move without melting, actual dance shoes, and yeah, deodorant became non-negotiable. I added mints to my bag and a sweat towel, little things that made a huge difference. Now? I move better, feel more confident, and haven't traumatized any partners with either wardrobe malfunctions or accidental aromatherapy.

I still bump into that dancer sometimes. She'll smile and say, "Got the right pants tonight?" And I'll grin back, "And a mint, too."

WHAT DO I WEAR

NEWBIE'S GUIDE TO CHOOSING WHAT TO WEAR

1. Prioritise Comfort First

If you're not comfortable, you won't be able to move freely. Choose clothes that let you stretch, twist, and spin without restriction.

2. Wear What Suits the Style

Each Latin style has its own vibe:

Salsa/Mambo: Fitted, breathable clothes for spins and turns

Bachata: Flowing or body-conscious attire for movement and connection

Reggaeton: Street-style, urban, relaxed

Samba: High-energy, vibrant, often with more flair

Match your outfit to the energy of the style.

3. Choose the Right Footwear

Invest in proper dance shoes with suede or leather soles. Avoid runners or sneakers with too much grip; they can strain your knees and limit movement.

4. Dress to Move, Not Impress

This isn't a fashion show, it's a dancing. Confidence comes from how you feel, not just how you look. Save the sequins for the stage.

5. Consider Partner Dancing

If you're in a partner class, avoid clothing that's too slippery, too oversized, or has too many straps, as it can get in the way during close contact.

6. Bring a Change of Shirt (Seriously)

Latin dance = sweat. If you're doing a double or heading to a social after class, a spare shirt will make you (and your dance partners) a lot more comfortable.

7. Keep Accessories Minimal

Dangling earrings, chunky bracelets, belts, or watches can become dangerous when spinning or doing partner work. Keep it simple and secure.

8. Be Mindful of Fragrance

Fresh is great, overpowering isn't. A clean shirt and some light deodorant go a long way on the dance floor.

9. Ask the School or Instructor

Different schools have different dress codes, especially for exams, performances, or intensives. If in doubt, ask!

10. Express Yourself, Gradually

As you grow in confidence, you'll find your style, maybe it's bold colours, fitted bodysuits, or classic black-on-black. Let your attire evolve with your journey.

Your outfit should support your dancing, not distract from it. Look good, feel great, and move freely, because confidence starts with comfort.

Can I Really Do This

So there I was, months into dancing, loving Salsa, hitting socials, even getting a few compliments here and there. But deep down, I knew something was off.

This is the part of my dance journey where I took a leap and booked my first private lesson.

At first, I thought privates were just for pros or competitors, not someone like me. I mean, I was doing okay in group classes, right? But every time I watched the really smooth dancers on the social floor, I could really see the difference. I'd ask myself, "How do they make it look so effortless?"

Admittedly, I was a little frustrated, all this time and effort, and I felt as though I just wasn't really improving.

One night after class, I stayed back and asked the instructor if they did privates. I half expected them to say no. Instead, they smiled and said, "Even if you feel you are not improving, trust the process, consistency will work for you, and YES, let's do it". That changed my frustration into anticipation as I believed the improvement I was waiting for was not far away..

That first session was a game changer. We broke down things I didn't even know I was doing wrong. My frame, my timing, even how I was leading. I got personalized tips, honest feedback, and drills that actually made a difference. It felt like the fog lifted.

It wasn't about perfection. It was about clarity. I could finally feel what the dance was supposed to be.

So, for anyone wondering if private lessons are "worth it." I've been there. And yeah, they totally are.

PRIVATE LESSONS

NEWBIE'S GUIDE TO CHOOSING PRIVATE DANCE LESSONS

1. Know Why You Want a Private

Are you looking to improve faster, prep for a comp, catch up on technique, or build confidence? Knowing your reason helps you and your instructor stay focused.

2. Choose the Right Instructor for You

Look for someone whose teaching style matches your learning style. Ask around, watch them in action, or book a trial to see if it clicks.

3. Ask About Their Specialties

Some instructors are amazing at fundamentals, others at choreography, performance, or partner connection. Make sure their strengths align with your goals.

4. Decide on Solo or Partner Focus

Do you want to work on solo skills like body movement and styling, or focus on lead/follow technique? Be clear from the start so the lesson is structured for you.

5. Budget for Progress

Private lessons are an investment. Some people take one as a booster, others do a series for consistent growth. Be realistic about what you can commit to.

6. Be Open About Your Level

You don't need to "prepare" for a private. Just show up as you are. A good instructor will meet you where you're at and build from there.

7. Ask About Feedback & Recap

Great privates often include personal corrections, drills, or even a short video recap. This helps you review and practice between sessions.

8. Studio or Zoom?

If you're far away or prefer learning from home, many instructors offer virtual privates. Ask about availability and how they structure online sessions.

9. Respect Their Time

Arrive early, warm up if needed, and communicate clearly. Treat it like a coaching session, because that's exactly what it is.

10. Track Your Growth

Keep a notebook or videos of what you've worked on. You'll be amazed how much progress you make over time—and it'll keep you motivated.

Private lessons are your shortcut to faster progress, deeper understanding, and personal breakthroughs.

What Am I Doing Here

I'd heard about Latin dance festivals, but I figured they were just for pros and performers. You know, the people doing 30 spins and splits on command. But then one of my dance friends said, "Dude, just come to one. It'll blow your mind."

This is the story of my very first Latin dance festival. I didn't really know what I was walking into. I bought a full pass, packed way too many shirts, and drove to the venue hoping I'd blend in. The lobby alone felt like a scene from a dance movie, heels clicking, music playing from every direction, people warming up like they were about to hit the Olympics of Salsa.

The first workshop I walked into was an Intermediate Salsa Workshop with an international artist I'd only seen on YouTube. Within five minutes, I was sweating bullets, spinning the wrong direction, and praying no one was watching. Spoiler: Everyone was too busy surviving to notice me.

I spent the first day bouncing from one overwhelming workshop to another. I was in over my head, and I knew it. That night, I almost didn't go to the social. I told myself I was tired. But deep down, I was intimidated. Still, I went.

And that night? That's when the magic happened. The social floor was full of dancers of all levels. Some were incredible, yes, but others were just there to connect, to enjoy the music, to dance. I found people who were happy to dance with a beginner, who smiled when I got something right, and laughed with me when I didn't. I stayed out way too late, forgot how tired I was, and danced with people from all over the world.

The next day, I skipped a couple of the crazy-hard workshops and chose beginner-friendly ones, Bachata footwork, Salsa shines, and body movement. I finally started having fun. By the end of the weekend, I was exhausted, inspired, and completely hooked. And guess what? I've been back every year since. I even ended up performing.

But more importantly, I realized festivals aren't just for the pros. They're for anyone who loves to dance and wants to have fun, be part of the larger community, and grow in the process. Here are some Latin dance festival tips, how to pick workshops, pace yourself, and avoid the "what am I doing here" spiral I went through. Get ready to get hooked!

DANCE FESTIVAL

NEWBIE'S GUIDE TO CHOOSING A GREAT FESTIVAL

1. Know Your Vibe: Party Animal or Precision Junkie?

Ask yourself:

Do you want to party all night or level up with intensive workshops? Looking for high-level competition, crazy socials, or non-stop shows?

Pro Tip: If you're a beginner, look for festivals that say "all levels welcome." If you're hardcore, hunt for "elite bootcamps" or "pro-level showcases."

2. Line-up Matters – A LOT

Check:

Which instructors are teaching?

Are your favorite performers or competitors on the roster?

Is it Latin-heavy or mixed with Urban, Kizomba, Bachata, etc.?

Red flag:

If no one on the flyer rings a bell, do some research or ask your dance friends.

3. Social Dancing: The Real Test

A great salsa festival means great socials.

Look for:

Dedicated Salsa rooms (not just Bachata with one Salsa track per hour). Quality DJs who understand musical flow. Clear start and end times (or better yet, NO end time!).

Bonus:

Festivals with live bands = chef's kiss.

4. Workshops That Work

You want: Well-structured workshop schedule

Variety: shines, partnerwork, technique, musicality. Classes are not overcrowded or jammed wall-to-wall

Pro Tip:

Read past attendee reviews – they'll tell you if the workshops were legit or just glorified selfies.

5. Location, Baby!

Is it easy to get to? Safe area?

Affordable food & accommodation nearby?

Is the venue new, world-class, comfortable, with good dance floors and, stage?

6. Size Matters: Large vs Small

Large festivals: See the whole dance community under one roof, massive line-ups, big energy, endless options, but you might feel lost in the crowd.

Small festivals: More connection, better access to artists, and often more personal vibes. You decide what suits you best.

7. Quality Shows

Ask around or search for past footage.

Do the shows run on time?

Are they endless or tight, and entertaining?

A well-produced show = a festival that respects your time.

8. Community Energy

Is the festival inclusive, welcoming, and friendly?

Do people support each other on and off the floor?

Festivals with good vibes are gold.

9. Reviews & Reputation

Before booking:

Ask trusted dancers, read comments on Instagram, FB groups, or YouTube, look at past event hashtags (#SalsaFestName2024)

10. Cost vs Value

What's included in the pass? Workshops? Socials? Shows? Bootcamps or Masterclasses? A cheaper pass might cost you more in add-ons. A pricier one might give you everything plus the kitchen sink.

The best salsa festivals leave you sweaty, smiling, and seriously inspired. If you come home with new friends, sore feet, and a hunger to dance more, you have chosen the right one.

This Is the New Me

I look back at where I started, and honestly, it feels like a lifetime ago.

I'm Nathan, and now, I dance almost every night of the week. Socials, classes, festivals, random spontaneous kitchen dance parties, you name it.

I've made incredible friends, found a community that feels like family, and yeah… I even found myself a partner. (Turns out, a good cross-body lead goes a long way.) But here's the thing: dancing didn't just change my nights. It changed my life.

I walk differently now, more grounded, more confident. I speak up more. I take up space in a way I didn't before. Dance taught me how to connect, how to listen, how to be present in the moment. It reminded me that it's okay to mess up, laugh it off, and keep moving. That rhythm exists not just in music, but in life.

The version of me who nervously showed up to his first class in stiff jeans and no rhythm wouldn't recognize this guy. And I love that.

So if you're reading this, wondering if you should try dancing, or if it's too late, or if you'll "be any good", go for it. You don't need to be perfect. You just need to start. The rest? It'll come. Step by step. Song by song. And here's something to help you out :)

Here is a list of all the questions I had when I started. The things no one tells you but everyone wonders. So whether you're brand new or just finding your way, you won't have to figure it all out alone.

Good luck, have fun, and welcome to our amazing dance world.

NEWBIES FAQS

QUICK QUESTIONS-QUICK ANSWERS

1. What should I wear to class?

Wear comfortable clothes you can move in—think workout or athletic wear. Avoid anything too baggy that might get in the way.

2. Do I need a partner?

Nope! Most group classes rotate partners, so you'll get to dance with different people and don't need to bring anyone.

3. What kind of shoes should I wear?

Lightweight shoes that stay on your feet and allow you to pivot work best. Dance shoes are ideal, but sneakers or flats with smooth soles are okay for beginners.

4. Do I need any dance experience?

Not at all! Beginner classes are designed for people with no prior experience. Just show up with a willingness to learn.

5. How long does it take to get good?

It depends on how often you practice, but with consistent effort, you'll start feeling confident in a few months. Everyone learns at their own pace!

6. Will I be the only beginner?

Definitely not. Beginners are always starting, and classes are structured with that in mind. You're not alone!

7. How often should I practice?

Even 15–30 minutes a few times a week can make a big difference. Practice regularly, and you'll see progress faster.

8. What's the difference between Salsa and Bachata (or other styles)?

Salsa is usually faster and more energetic, while Bachata is slower and more sensual. Each has its own music, steps, and vibe—try both and see what you like!

9. How do I improve my timing and rhythm?

Listen to the music often and count the beats when you dance. Over time, your body will naturally start to feel the rhythm.

10. What if I have two left feet?

Everyone starts somewhere! Feeling uncoordinated is normal at first, but with practice, you will improve.

11. How do I remember the steps?

Repetition is key. Practice new moves slowly at first, and don't be afraid to ask your instructor to review something again.

12. Should I lead or follow?

Traditionally, men lead and women follow, but you can choose whatever role you prefer—many dancers learn both!

13. Can I go social dancing as a beginner?

Absolutely! Social dancing is for all levels. People are usually very welcoming and understanding of beginners.

14. What if I mess up on the dance floor?

No worries—it happens to everyone! Just smile, keep moving, and enjoy the music. Most partners won't even notice or care.

15. How do I ask someone to dance?

Just smile and say, "Would you like to dance?" Most people will say yes! Being polite and friendly goes a long way.

16. Is it okay to say no to a dance?

Yes, it's always okay to say no—just be kind about it. And if someone says no to you, don't take it personally.

17. How do I avoid stepping on toes (literally and figuratively)?

Focus on a good frame and timing. Also, be respectful—don't criticize your partner or give unsolicited advice.

18. When will I be ready for performances or competitions?

When you feel confident and your instructor thinks you're ready. Everyone's journey is different—there's no rush!

19. Should I take private lessons?

Private lessons can really accelerate your progress, especially if you want focused feedback. But they're not required to enjoy dancing.

20. What are the best ways to progress faster?

Practice consistently, take classes regularly, go social dancing, and don't be afraid to make mistakes—that's how you grow.

My Love Story

"My Love Story" is a heartfelt, humorous, and insightful journey through the eyes of Nathan, a newcomer who discovers the transformative world of Latin dancing. What begins as a casual attempt to boost confidence and meet new people quickly evolves into a life-changing passion.

The story unfolds in chapters that mirror key stages of a beginner's dance journey. Choosing a dance school, finding a preferred style, selecting the right clothing, venturing into socials and festivals, and investing in private lessons. Each experience is shared with relatable anecdotes, some awkward, some triumphant, but all rich with practical tips and emotional truths.

Nathan's narrative blends personal growth with dance education. From the panic of his first social to the confidence built through private lessons, he offers guidance on how to avoid common pitfalls and find joy in the process. The booklet doubles as a comprehensive guide for dance newbies, including top-10 lists for choosing schools, styles, socials, festivals, what to wear, and more. It also shares 20 FAQs for new dancers starting their journey, no matter where you are in the world.

Ultimately, the story is about more than dance. It's about community, self-expression, resilience, and transformation.

Nathan's closing reflection, how dancing changed not just his nights, but his entire outlook, offers a powerful message: anyone can find their rhythm and their people, one step at a time.

About The Author

Jaime Jesus is a renowned Latin dance professional and an inspiring community leader whose influence has touched thousands of lives around the world. With an unshakable passion for Salsa and Bachata, Jaime has spent decades not only mastering the art of dance but using it as a powerful tool for transformation, connection, and empowerment. Through his work as a performer, instructor, event organizer, and mentor, Jaime has opened doors for countless individuals, helping them find confidence, joy, and purpose on and off the dance floor. Known for his authenticity, dedication, and heart-led leadership, Jaime has helped shape the Latin dance community into a more inclusive, vibrant, and united space. My Love Story is more than a story of personal journey, it's a tribute to the lives changed through rhythm, movement, and love, and a celebration of the profound impact the Latin Dance Community offers worldwide, and how it welcomes everyone who wants to be part of it.